Written by Joanne Langlois ★ Paintings by Heather Haynes

D1299210

I'm a GREAT me!
Another Bethie Adventure

Toni

Wherever I go and whoever I See,

There's Brucie, my brother, with eyes **BIG** and **Blue**.
He's lucky to have them, my Mum's got 'em too.

There's Hazel, my friend, with a halo of curls.
Her hair is the envy of all little girls.

My hair is *so* straight, as STRAIGHT as can be.
I can put it in a braid, but that's it for me.

There's Billy, the boy at the front of the class.
He can run like the wind. He can run super *FAST*.

I can run too, but not quite like him.
I try not to stand too **CLOSE** during gym.

There's Lucy, the girl with a home like a **CASTLE**.
Whatever **she** wants, she gets... with no hassle.

MY house is quite nice, it has what I need,
but to get what I want, I must beg! I must plead!

There's Lily from *dance* class, who does pirouettes.
She pliés and sashays, and knows she's the BEST.

I *Love* to do dance, but I can be quite a sight. Sometimes I mistake my **LEFT** and my **RIGHT**!

I'd L♥VE to sing, to belt out a tune,
but whenever I try, dogs howl at the M☺☺N!

There's Hannah, my sister... a BABY, to boot.
She just has to sit there, and boy is she cute!

There's the girl on the bus, with the coat like a LEOPARD, called Annalise Lulubelle Marguerite Sheppard.

I am Elisabeth, but Bethie's my name.
It's not very fancy, in fact, it's quite plain.

I may not run fast, or sing right on key, or dance on my toes, but I love being me.

I know that I'm special. There's LOTS I can do!
I can **skate**! I can **swim**! I can **bicycle** too!

I love to draw people and **fish** with their gills, **rainbows** and sunsets and houses on hills.

I'm a really good friend, just ask Betty Lou.
There's a game that I taught her, to stop feeling blue.

"Just look at Beth's smile!", I've heard people say.
"She can **brighten** a room, not to mention one's day."

And I try to be nice, even to Rick,

who sometimes says “Hi”, wit h a swift little Kick.

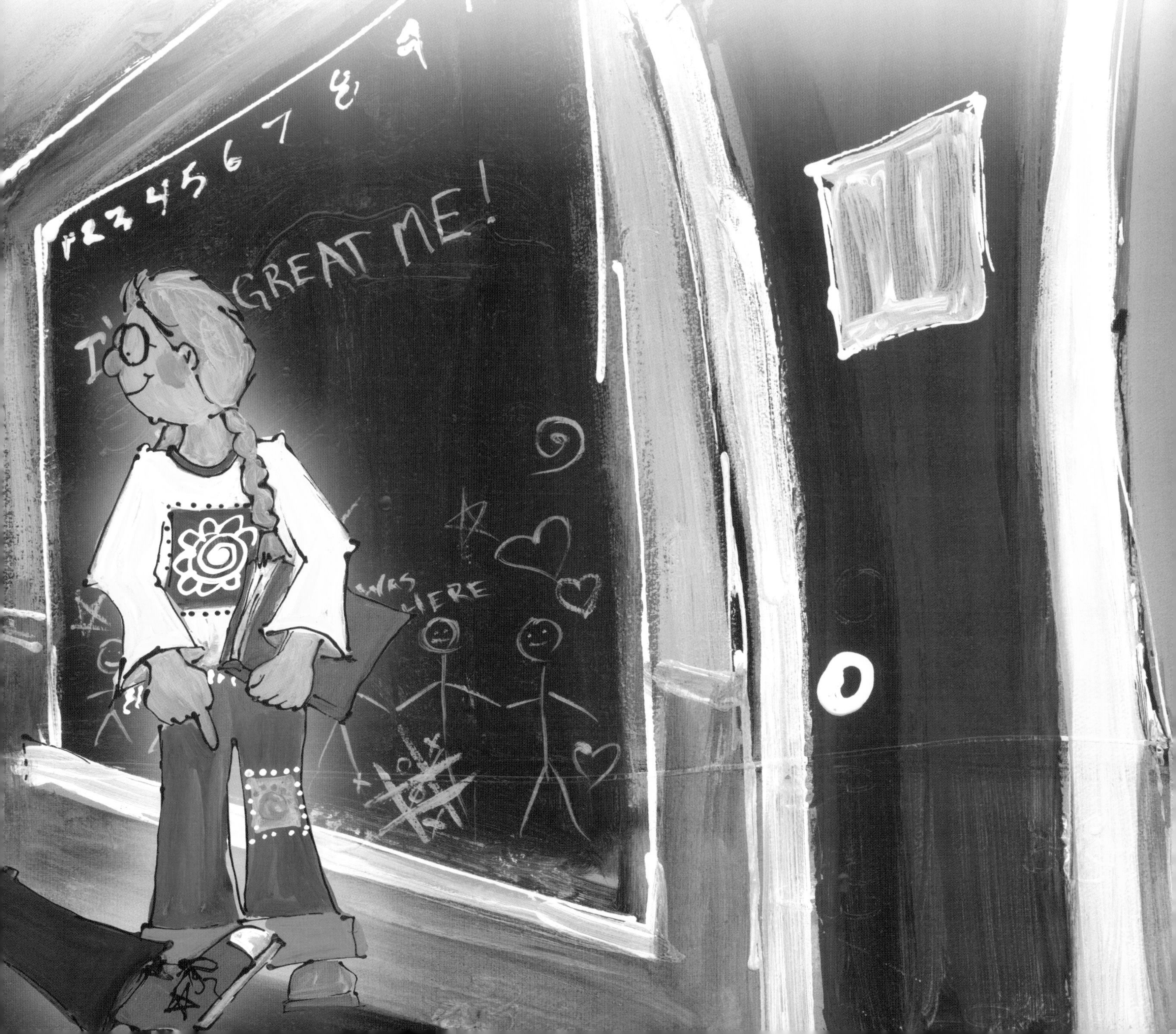

But what I do  , is just being me!
Who could do better? No one that *I See*!

I like that I'm different, and not quite the same, as him or as her, or as… what's-his-name.

I may not be perfect, as I'm sure you can see,
but one thing I know, is that...

I'm a **GREAT** me!

To help children to like themselves and to help build self-esteem, <u>all</u> children must be given the tools to feel that they are GREAT!

To open a conversation after reading the story, try asking the child some of the following questions:

What do you like about you?
Tell me five things that you like about yourself.

What do your friends like about you?
What do you like about your friends?

Why do we need friends?
Do you have a best friend?

What is it about that person that makes him / her so special?

Talk about why Bethie liked herself.

Discuss the characters in the story and what Bethie liked about each.

What part of the story did you like best and why?

Why is it important to like yourself for who you are?

Do you compare yourself to your friends?

What is the one thing you would like to be able to do?
(It's probably possible - it just takes practice!)

How did this book make you feel?
What did you like best about the book?

What character is most like you?